P9-CEA-440
DISCARDED

Waiting to Waltz

Waiting to Waltz
A Childhood

Poems by Cynthia Rylant

Drawings by Stephen Gammell

A Richard Jackson Book
Atheneum Books for Young Readers
New York London Toronto Sydney Singapore

To Gerry and our life on Hawthorne

CONTENTS

BEAVER

Coming to it from the country,
proud that I finally had sidewalks to walk
and indoor plumbing.
Little strip of street called Beaver:
Hardware, laundromat, market,
post office, Kool-Kup, and Moon-Glo motel.
Beaver Creek holding it all together,
and me on the edge.
Like the water, muddy and rolling.
Growing in Beaver.

WAX LIPS

Todd's Hardware was dust and a monkey—
a real one, on the second floor—
and Mrs. Todd there behind the glass cases.
We stepped over buckets of nails and lawnmowers
to get to the candy counter in the back,
and pointed at the red wax lips,
and Mary Janes,
and straws full of purple sugar.
Said goodbye to Mrs. Todd, she white-faced and silent,
and walked the streets of Beaver,
our teeth sunk hard in the wax,
and big red lips worth kissing.

THE BRAIN SURGEON

The drunks liked to sit beside Beaver Creek
and one drunk in particular was handsome.
Dirty and needed a shave, but handsome.
And because of it I thought surely he was
a tragic figure
and determined that, in fact, he was
a Brain Surgeon
whose wife had died their honeymoon night
in the Moon-Glo motel
as they were passing through to Florida.
So he checked out and sat beside Beaver Creek
and now would never leave it.

GENERAL DELIVERY

We got our mail
General Delivery
at the Beaver Post Office.
That meant our house had
no number
and no street.
And we couldn't afford
to rent a box.
Just General Delivery.
Still,
it was nice
being big enough in Beaver
that folks could send you mail
care of The Town,
and you were known.

MR. LAFON

Our landlord was Mr. Lafon.
Mr. Lafon's jaws were flabby and he wore
thick glasses and teetered a little.
Still, he could step into white coveralls,
lower a net across his face,
and walk into a thousand bees.
He fell asleep in the church choir
and never drove a car
but he was a man of singular courage.

LITTLE SHORT LEGS

Little black dog
down the road
we called
Little Short Legs.
One day
my mother late for work
went driving hard
down that dirt road.
Ran over Little Short Legs.
Never knew a grown-up could
make such a mistake.
Never knew one could make it
and say it was so
and feel sorry.
But she did.
And nothing for me to say
but
it's all right, Mom.
It's all right.

HOLINESS

I had a Holiness babysitter
who rolled my hair off my forehead like hers
and took me in the church bus on Sundays
to the Pentecostal church.
And there people prayed aloud and never at the same time
and shook tambourines
with eyes shut tight, hallelujah.
And on the church bus back
I looked out the window, away from her,
because I didn't understand
such noise
and was frightened
by God.

SPELLING BEE

Best speller since third grade
that Beaver Elementary
had ever seen.
Could spell assassination
when I was nine.
When I was eleven
entered the
Big Spelling Bee.
Winning would mean
a try at the
county championship
and then—the world.
Everyone knew I'd win.
But first, I had to
win at Beaver.
Nervous beyond words,
I was asked to spell
woke.
Sputtered W-O-A-K.
WOAK.
Knew I'd blown it,
just nervous,
but made them check a
dictionary, anyway,
to save myself some
dignity
and on the chance that
some stupid idiot
like me
had used it in a
spelling bee
and made it
a word.
It wasn't.

THE GREAT BEYOND

Karen Ward had a
concrete swimming pool
in her yard.
Went up one Saturday
to swim,
never telling anyone
I didn't know how
except in a hole
not too deep.
Halfway across
the eight-foot end
started to sink.
Half dog-paddled and
half plain walked on water
to reach
the other side.
And no one ever knew,
not even Karen,
how close I'd come
to the great beyond.

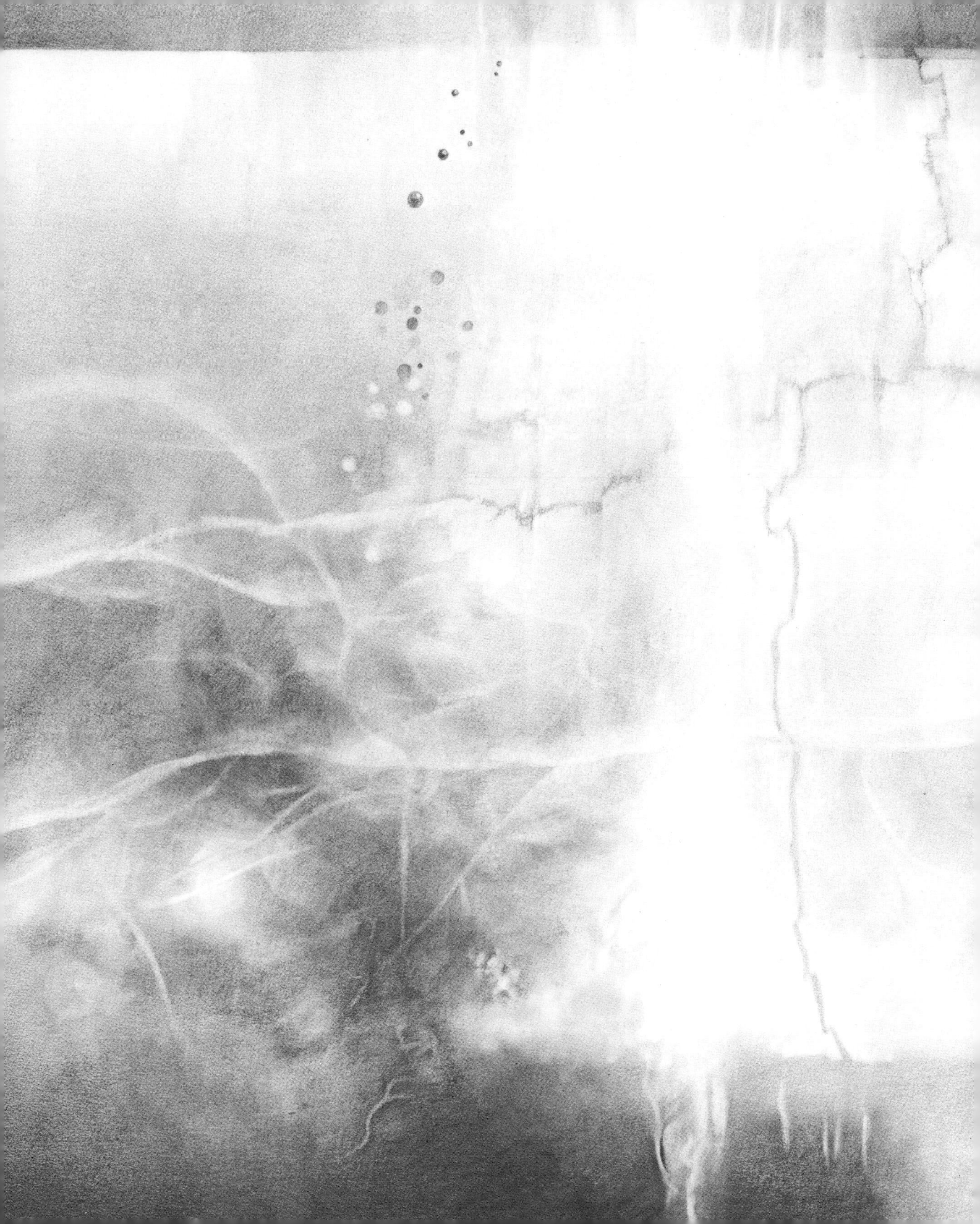

HENRY'S MARKET

At Henry's Market you could charge things—
like a bottle of strawberry pop—
to your family's bill
and when you paid Henry
at the end of the month,
he gave you a bag full of candy bars you could
choose yourself.
Henry's old father lived next to the store
and stood in his shorts on the porch sometimes,
offering bananas to kids who walked by.
But no one ever took one
because he was just too weird.

THE RESCUE

Running down the tracks one day,
thunder and lightning coming up on me,
and there a little girl crying
and walking,
looking at the sky.
Me scared to death of storms
crossing over:
You going home? Want me to walk with you?
And turning away from my house to walk her
through Beaver
to hers.
Lightning and thunder strong now.
So there's her mother on the porch, waving,
and she says bye to me then runs.
I turn around
and walk in the storm
slow and straight,
but inside,
a little girl crying.

CASSIUS

Cassius was our gray and white tom
who stayed on the prowl.
On a Sunday night my mother saw
what looked to be a squashed cat
on the highway.
Gray and white.
Scooped it into a paper bag
and gave it a proper burial.
Poor Cassius.
So we were sad for Cassius
a while
then stopped thinking of him.
One morning, six o'clock,
a meow at the front door
and there was Cassius.
We had to laugh.
Who was that
my mother
scooped?

SWEARING

For a year had
a best friend named Randy.
Japanese American
who liked to play Tarzan.
And Randy and I
used to say
"I swear to God"
when we were shocked,
amused, annoyed, or
just plain bored.
No one ever told us
not to
until one day
a lady
said it was wrong.
We were plainly surprised
at the revelation
and wondered why
no one
ever told us before.
After all, we were
just a couple of kids, we said.
I swear to . . . .
Rats.

SAM THE SHOE SHOP MAN

Sam owned the Beaver Shoe Shop.
Dumpy little business in a one-room building
the size of a garage.
Big picture window, though, and cat calendars.
And Randy and I swung back that old screen door
every day all summer,
the smell of leather hitting us square in the face
and melting us through.
We sat in the shoe-shine chairs
and talked with Sam for hours,
admiring his bald head and hairy arms
and never once guessing he was poor.
Never once.

MAD DOG

Saw a movie about a girl in a Southern town
who dressed up like a ham for a play
and nearly got killed.
And whose father shot down
a mad dog in the street.
Mad dog jerking up the street
in that movie.
And for weeks after,
afraid to walk through Lafon's yard
to the bus stop every morning,
thinking some mad dog
there
jerking around the corner.
And no father with a gun
to shoot it down.

MR. DILL

Living over a garage
next to us,
strange Mr. Dill.
Funny name, but
nobody laughed.
Because Mr. Dill stood
straight and tall,
wore a smart hat,
and spoke fast and sharp.
Mr. Dill living all alone
and buying my seeds
and my lemonade
and my greeting cards.
And driving off one day
in his little red car,
I guess.
No one noticed
until maybe
three years later.
Sorry, Mr. Dill.

THE KOOL-KUP

In the summer every day
I walked down to the Kool-Kup.
Had a dollar
for a chili dog, chips, and shake.
Nobody at home
to make me lunch.
Chili dogs and cheeseburgers
all summer long
until I was sick of them.
But I never let on.
Because I could have gotten
a fat old babysitter
who ate rum candy
while she watched the soaps.
Locking me out of the house
'til five.
Or worse—
I might have been told
to make my own lunch.

PINK BELLY

They said don't go to the playground after school
because the boys are giving pink bellies.
And the girls were afraid
and stayed home,
for the school was right in front
of Sheriff Wickline's house
and it was rumored his son Jimmy
was leading the pink belly bunch
so what hope was there
for a girl
in Beaver?

PTA

Seemed like everybody's mother
went to PTA
but mine.
Mine just died every day
after work.
Cathy's mom served popcorn
at the ballgames and
Carolyn's mom made the cheerleading
uniforms.
But mine fell asleep during
the Christmas play.
Wishing my mom
were in PTA.
Until one day a boy
fainted
in class
and everyone turned to me
and said
what do we do?
Because my mom
was a nurse
and they knew it, and she might never
pop popcorn at halftime
but she could
sure
save their lives, boy.
PTA could just
keep her
on call.

MIKE AND MAJOR

Mike's sister said he
listened to Lawrence Welk records
and cried.
But it didn't matter to me.
Mike rode a 10-speed bike
when they were still called
English.
And he had a collie dog
named Major.
Major so majestic
trotting beside that
English bicycle.
Understanding Beaver
better than us all.
Mike loved The Beatles, too.
So we listened together,
us three.
Major finally grew old
and one day didn't see
a car.
Mike all alone on his bike.
Carrying that pain
until
he could
drive.

FORGOTTEN

Mom came home one day
and said my father had died.
Her eyes all red.
Crying for some stranger.
Couldn't think of anything to do,
so I walked around Beaver
telling the kids
and feeling important.
Nobody else's dad had died.
But then
nobody else's dad had worn
red-striped pajamas
and nobody else's dad had made
stuffed animals talk
and nobody else's dad had gone away
nine years ago.
Nobody else's dad had been so loved
by a four-year-old.
And so forgotten by one
now
thirteen.

BAND PRACTICE

Joined the band.
Ronnie-next-door played trombone
so I took up trumpet.
Never once considered a clarinet
or flute.
Not thinking, at eleven,
what a girl looks like
playing trumpet.
Didn't think about it until
I was thirteen.
So I tried out for majorette
to march in front:
tassled boots,
painted legs,
and a smile.
Made it.
Forgot a lot about playing
trumpet.
Learned a lot
about
playing.

CATHOLICS

Sue Halstead was a rich girl.
Her mother wore bikinis
and made mixed drinks
and had white-rimmed glasses.
In Beaver.
Sue had a party one Friday
and invited some Catholics
from Beckley.
I'd never met Catholics before.
Catholic boys with slick
black hair
in her house.
Me in the corner
knowing
they were rich
and that they crossed themselves
when they prayed.
Wanting to be Catholic.
Wanting to be Catholic, please God,
and cross myself
and kneel
with the
slick-haired
boys.

SM

STEVE

Steve Meador moving to Beaver
the summer before sixth grade.
And when school started
me stuck with him in a split-grade
when everybody who was
important
went into the purely Sixth Grade room.
Shriveled old teacher
and half a room of
ten year olds to deal with,
that's what I got.
But Steve and I became friends.
And we were king and queen
of split-grade,
Archie and Veronica.
But Steve moved away after a year.
Came back two years later.
Me wearing bras then
and I'd gotten kissed.
Ignored Steve because
his voice was funny
and his lips too fat.
Lost him.
And really forever.
Growing.

<u>JIMMY'S DAD</u>

Jimmy's dad worked for
the Beaver Block Company
and he was not married.
Jimmy and I
were sort of sweethearts
in seventh grade
and I used to worry.
Because his dad was
the only unmarried man
I knew
and maybe
the only one my mother knew.
So if they got married
Jimmy and I would be
related
and living with them
in that little white house
across from Beaver Block.
However,
Jimmy's dad
had the personality
of a fish, I soon discovered,
and my mom
was no fool,
thank the Lord.

PET ROCK

Roger came to Beaver
and fell in love
with me.
Big gorilla boy
with long arms
and a confused look.
Proved his devotion
by sitting on the couch
for hours
reading all my comics.
After a while
I learned to accept him
like a piece of furniture.
And lived my life
as if he weren't there.
Occasionally offered him
food and drink,
unsure how long love
could sustain him.
And when Pet Rocks became popular,
decided I didn't
need one, really,
having Roger.

ROCKY TRAILER'S GRANDMOTHER'S GARAGE

I had a friend named Jo who wanted
always to be good.
So when I started hanging out
at Rocky Trailer's grandmother's garage
to listen to his band practicing,
Jo called them a bunch of hoods.
But how could she have understood
how an electric guitar
could change a boy
for a girl who loved
Paul McCartney?

SAVED

At fourteen I went regularly to Beaver Baptist
because I wanted to play piano there someday
and going was a start.
One Sunday dragged my mother there.
The preacher was heated up
and talked about hell more than I could bear.
Screamed I was a tree before God:
Would I stand... or would I FALL?
And while the choir sang Just As I Am,
just as I was I went up the aisle
and told him I was a sinner.
Seven other sinners came up behind.
After church all of us shaking hands, tears pouring,
and my mother embarrassed,
surely wishing she'd stayed in bed,
for she'd never liked preachers
who yelled people to the Cross.
Dismayed her daughter could be so duped.

TEENAGERS

Watching the teenagers
in Beaver
using hairspray and
lipstick.
Kissing at ballgames.
Going steady.
And wanted it fast,
wanted it now.
Because all my pretend
had to be hidden.
All my games
secret.
Wanted to be a wide-open child
but too big,
too big.
No more.
Waiting to shave
and wear nylons
and waltz.
Forgetting when
I was last time
a child.
Never knowing
when it
ended.

THE WORLD

Went to Florida once—
New York, too.
Going out of Beaver to the world.
Left it all behind
and lied about what it really was.
Lied about Beaver.
And came back with a tan
and with cheap jewelry,
but no one really cared
about what I'd seen.
And I didn't know
who I was
anymore.
Just knew my dreams
would fill up Beaver Creek.
Fill it up and go rolling,
go rolling on down Beaver Creek,
rolling on down
to the world.

Atheneum Books for Young Readers
An imprint of Simon & Schuster Children's Publishing Division

Original Simon & Schuster Books for Young Readers edition, 1984
Revised format edition, January 2001

 The text of this book is set in 12 pt. Goudy Old Style. The illustrations are pencil drawings reproduced in halftone.

Manufactured in China 10 9 8 7 6 5 4

Library of Congress Cataloging in Publication Data Rylant, Cynthia. Waiting to waltz, a childhood. Summary: A cycle of thirty poems chronicles a young girl's growing up in a small Appalachian town. 1. Children's poetry, American. [1. Appalachian region — Poetry. 2. American poetry] I. Gammell, Stephen, ill. II. Title PS3568.Y55W3 1984 811'.54 84-11030
ISBN 0-689-84292-9